Grandy Goose Rhymes
by
Elaine H. Leone

A foible
is an endearing or charming weakness
in character or behavior.

Book design and illustrations by:
Elaine H. Leone and Scott T. Leone

Printed in the United States of America

ISBN # 978-1-4675-6477-9
1. Juvenile Fiction/Poetry
2. Juvenile Fiction/Family/General

Visit us at TheGrandies.com

Dedication

To Tom, Scott, Duffy, Lizabeth,
Andrea, Eliza, Anna, Noah,
Alexandra and Peter Leone

From my heart to yours...

Table of Contents.

Introduction

To Nana and Nanny
To Grandma and Granny
To Grandfather, Grandad and Pappy,
Read with the children at your knee.
Grandieland is the place to be
Where everybody is happy.

Uncle Ted

When we need a sitter,
We hope it's Uncle Ted
Because he doesn't make up rules
Or make us go to bed.
We make believe we're rock stars
And play the music loud
And we jump around and holler
Like the teeny bopper crowd
But the last time ....
Mom came home at midnight
And we STILL were not in bed
And Uncle Ted was dancing
With a lampshade on his head
So Mom says ....
"No more Uncle Ted.
It's Grandma Mary Lou instead."

Know—How

Grandy tried so hard to get
The car seat hooked up tight.
She mumbled and she grumbled
But she couldn't get it right.
My little cousin rolled his eyes
And grinned as Grandy blew it.
He then announced, to her surprise,
"Don't worry. I can do it."

Amen

When I sneezed, "ACHOO!"
Tess said, "God bless YOU!"
Then I sneezed and sneezed again.
She blessed. I sneezed.
She blessed. I sneezed.
She stared at me and then
She said, "I'm going to go and play.
I can't keep blessing YOU all day!"

Grateful Ned

Mom makes me eat my vegetables
But Grandy likes to please.
She doesn't cook the broccoli,
She makes me mac and cheese.
When Mom reminds her of the greens
And puts her on the spot,
Grandy says she's getting old
And that she just forgot.
(wink, wink)

The Infatuated Cat

My pretty Aunt Lizzie is now fully grown
So now she has moved to a place of her own
But a neighborhood cat has her in a tizzy.
He just sits on her porch
And stares at Aunt Lizzie.

Star Gazer

When I look at the stars at night,
I strain my eyes to see
If there is somebody up there
Looking back at me.

Talking Turkey

"Gobble, gobble, gobble,"
Was all Bobby had to say
When he was the turkey
In the school Thanksgiving play.
The Pilgrims and the Indians
Chased and overtook him
And, though he gobbled very loud,
In Act II, they cooked him.

California Carnival

Patsy and Penny and Julie and Jenny
Rode on a Ferris wheel.
When they got to the top
And it came to a stop,
You could have heard them squeal
In South Dakota.

Mt. Hushmore

The Model Kit (With 100 Pieces)

Thank you for helping me build the plane.
It seemed an impossible task.
You just came along and helped with it
Without my having to ask.
It's standing now in a special place
Upon my bedroom shelf.
Somehow you just knew it-
That I just couldn't do it
Myself.
You are a very good grandfather.

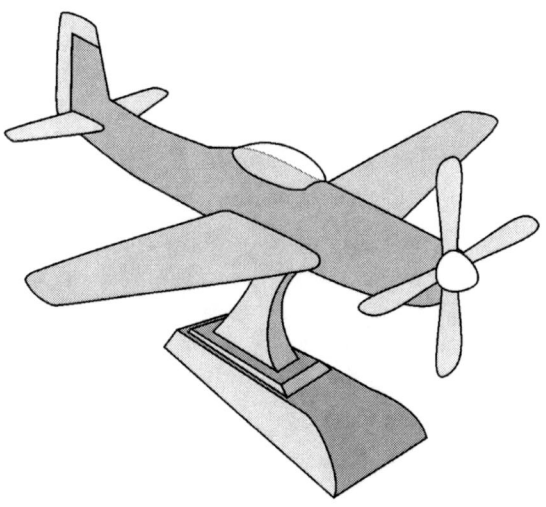

Kelly

Our baby cousin's Kelly Hatch.
No kid is as cute as Kelly
But she chews on chives in the onion patch
And she smells like the corner deli.

Dirty Trix

It had rained for days and days
And there were lots of puddles
So Trixie made some mud pies
And she called them "mushy muddles".
Grandy let her mix the mud
For about an hour
Then she dragged her in the house
And stuck her in the shower.

Grandy Says:

When you get a birthday gift
From your Great-Aunt Kate, it
Is a good idea to let her know
That you appreciate it
And say that it works very well
(Even if it won't)
And say you like it very much
(Even if you don't).

The Gymnasts

The Tucker twins did jumping jacks
And exercised for fun.
The Burton boys, while watching them,
Were not to be outdone.
They leaped out of an apple tree
And, landing on their feet,
They did a couple of jumping jacks
AND cartwheeled down the street.
Another neighbor kid named Fred
Stayed in his yard and stood on his head.

Dogdom

Any boy that's named Nathaniel
Should probably own a cocker spaniel
And, if that's the case, then Jason Weaver
Should have a Labrador retriever
But I guess a boy named Augie
Can have any kind of doggie.

Losing Their Grippe

Scott and Duffy had the flu
With very stuffy heads
And so, for a day or two,
They lay in their twin beds.
The boys were really very sick
And their heads were hot.
They couldn't do arithmetic
And fell asleep a lot.
Then ...
They got into a pillow fight
(and Duffy met his match).
They broke the bulb in the reading light
When they started playing catch.
When they wrestled on the floor
And overturned the stool,
Mother opened up the door
And they went back to school.

Saint Peter

Pete's been kind of naughty lately
So Grandy says to lay low
And take a little extra time
To polish up his halo.

The Rainy Train

Sometimes when it is thundering
Or just about to rain,
We line up chairs in the dining room
And make The Rainy Train.
I'm usually the passenger,
Complete with all my gear.
Chuck is the conductor
And Lynn's the engineer.
We blow the whistle and we chug
Like locomotives do
And pretend our destination
Is the San Diego Zoo
But if the weather changes
And it really *doesn't* rain,
Then I say I have no ticket
And they toss me off the train
Because if the sun is shining,
We can just go back outside
And on a different rainy day,
We'll take another ride.

Bar Exam
(or Passing the Bar)

Should I buy the candy bar
And eat it right away
Or save up my allowance
For something else some day?
If I save week after week
(Forget the candy bar),
Maybe I can save enough
To buy myself a car…
Or a skateboard.

save   spend

The Right Slant

While trying to do backbends,
It occurred to Jill
That
It might be easier if she
Did backbends on a hill.

Thanksgiving

The kitchen smells delicious
And dinner time is near.
The cousins, aunts and uncles
And the grandparents are here.
The turkey's on the table
And Dad will do the carving.
We wish that he would hurry up ...
Everybody's starving.

Motherly Shove

Doug and I kept arguing
' til Mom put down her broom
And, with her hands upon her hips,
Sent each one to his room.
We sat there in our doorways
Rolling trucks to one another
And, with real comraderie,
Complained about our mother.

Victoria

Victoria's such an elegant name,
A name fit for a queen.
Nobody named Victoria
Could ever be cross or mean.
I only know one Victoria
And that is Victoria Grant.
Whenever she has a picnic,
You don't see a single ant.
Her clothes are always tidy.
You don't see a single spot.
Whenever she writes a letter,
You don't see a single blot.
Victoria's always perfect.
Her footprints leave no tracks.
When she gets too picky,
We call her Vicky
And give her a chance to relax.

Riley

Riley Reed ate a *pumpkin seed*
And became a nervous fella.
He worried he'd grow up to be
A coach for Cinderella.

Easy Driver

There's a car attached to the grocery cart.
Though Steve can't steer or park it,
He likes being in the driver's seat
And cruising around the market.

Fly Swatter

That fly kept buzzing 'round my head.
I swung at her and missed her.
I meant to swat the fly instead
But ...
I swatted my little sister.
I *knew* that fly meant trouble.

heh heh

Jorja

At my sister's dance recital,
In the part that was ballet,
I saw a ballerina
Whose name was Jorja Shay.
She wore a silver tutu
With silver stars and bows
And, in her silver slippers,
She danced upon her toes.
I didn't mean to stare at her
But couldn't look away
And I decided then and there
To marry Jorja Shay
Some day.

Role Model (not)

Grandy says that grandmothers
All bore her half to death
When they talk about their grandchildren
With every other breath
But I notice Grandy holds her own
And won't give them a chance.
She says I'm bright and beautiful
And they should see me dance.
She says that I am very smart
But, then, so is my brother
And Mommy gets embarrassed
And she says, "Now, *MOTHER!*"

Unlisted

Mom's friends have really unusual names.
Judy Nextdoor is neat.
Then there's Judy Debbiessister
And Judy Acrossthestreet.

Colors

Yellow's always sunshine
Green is Mother's eyes.
Blue is sky and sailor suits
And red is cherry pies.
Purple is my Uncle Newt
In his purple bathing suit.

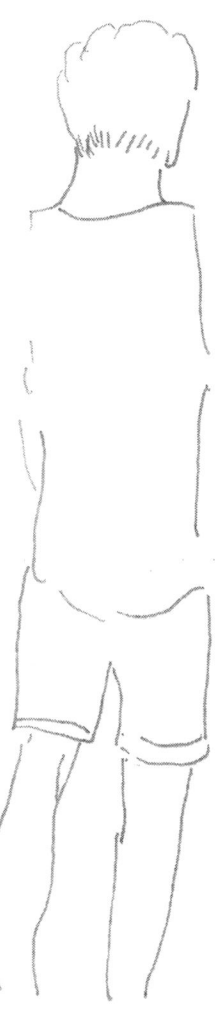

Color
bathing
suit
purple

Night Life

I travel to exotic ports.
I medal in Olympic sports.
I ride a horse on a western plain.
I sail a ship on the bounding main.
I wish those memories would keep
Of all I do while I'm asleep.
I wish those memories would stay
But they disappear with the break of day
And I'm half in a dream that I half forgot.
Oh, what is real and what is not?
Then I hear Mom call, "It's school time, Neal."
And I know exactly what is real.

Foreign Exchange

When Herr Hinkel asked,
"Sprechen sie Deutsch?",
He gave me a big wink so
I knew he wouldn' t be upset
When I said, "I don' t think so."

Do you speak German?

Five Kittens

Mary Lee and Michael Souza
Named their kitten *Lalapalooza*.
Three-year-old Sabrina Bly
Named her kitten *Cutie Pie*.
Christopher and Joey Hurley
Named their two kittens
Moe and *Curly*.

OUR kitten's a little detective,
Always searching for a clue.
She sniffs and snoops around so much
That we named her *Nancy Drew*.

Ghost Story (maybe)

Maxine Tyler likes to boast
That once she really saw a ghost.
Since that night was Halloween,
We all knew it was Jeffrey Green.
He couldn't wait to scare Maxine.

The Crankies

Sometimes they just sneak up on Rhett.
He had a bad day in math
Or he didn't get his allowance yet
Or he had to take a bath.

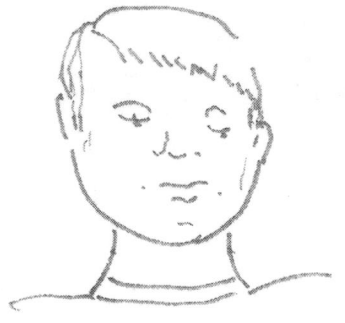

Trade Secret

I didn't like my sandwich
So I made a deal with Shelley
And traded her my tuna fish
For peanut butter/jelly.
I made her promise me that she
Wouldn't tell my brother
Because I knew for sure that he
Would go and tell my mother.

The Assignment

"Think of your Grandad," teacher said.
"What word comes first to mind?"
Joan said, "Garden." Jeff said, "Golf."
Jacqueline said, "Kind."
Jim said, "Football." Tim said, "Tall."
Mary Jo said, "Train."
Ted said, "Brave." Fred said, "Shave."
Isabel said, "Cane."
Pam said, "Smoke." Sam said, "Joke".
Pat said, "Pussycat."
Dan said, "Chef." Dave said, "Deaf."
Ben said, "Democrat."
Phil said, "Pains." Bill said, "Brains."
Callie Dunn said, "Funny."
John said, "Couch." Ron said, "Grouch"
And Madison said, "Money."

When she asked about Grandy,
I said, "Hugs"
And Gwen said, "Oriental rugs."

Grandy Says:

If you don't know
And you let it go,
Later on it will always show.
Don't wear a mask
And pretend you know.
Ask.
Puzzled?
Don't be muzzled.
Ask.

Chad

As they left for their vacation,
An excited little Chad
Asked at every other stoplight,
"Are we there yet, Dad?"

The Oral Report

My book report was on *Moby Dick*,
A very exciting tale
Of Captain Ahab and his crew
And their search for the great white whale.

When Moby Dick bit the boat in half,
One of the boys had a nervous laugh
But I guess ...
The girls thought he would chew the crew up
Because Abbie cried, "Oh, Oh, Oh, NO!"
And Pammie threw up.

Brett

If we upset little cousin, Brett,
He stares at us and scowls.
When we try to make UP, he
Acts like the puppy
And sits on the floor and growls.

The Good Fairy

They were playing make-believe
But they didn't get along.
Kerry, the good fairy, said
That Nate was always wrong
And that he couldn't be the king.
When he asked the reason why,
She hit him with her magic wand
And gave him a black eye.

He told his friends he got the shiner
Playing ball behind the diner.

Wiggle Room

These shoes are too tight.
They are crushing my toes.
I don't care if it rains.
I don't care if it snows.
These shoes are going
Right back in the box
And I'm wearing my sandals
(Or sandals with sox)
Or I may just go barefoot
The rest of my life
And live on a beach
With my barefooted wife.

Nell

Jennifer Lilly knows it's silly
To run after Nellie Thatcher.
Nell runs as fast as Wingfoot Willie
And even *he* can't catch her.

King James

When Jamie Ward gets feeling bored
And bosses us all about,
Grandy says, "Oh, yes, My Lord,"
And then James cuts it out.

Caroline

Caroline Cassandra Tate
Doesn't know about paying bills
Or about the cost of real estate.
She wants to move to Beverly Hills.
She'd like a pony, a swimming pool,
A maid, a mansion, a fancy car.
To Caroline, it would be cool
To live the life of a movie star.
Well, to Grandy, it wasn't funny.
She hates to see a bubble burst.
She said, "Well, Honey, save your money
And finish kindergarten first."

Taste Buddies

Peanut butter and cheese are nice.
They taste good to kids and mice.

Car Trick

Dad called us all to the garage,
"Come, someone left a mule!"
But there was only Daddy's Dodge
And he said, "April fool!"

The Voters

Brothers (two) and Betsy Lee
Altogether that makes three.
It makes the boys the majority.
Do you know what that means
In a democracy?
It means there is no way
Betsy can win.

Ballot	
☐	One Thing
☐	The Other Thing

Totals	
Betsy Lee	Brothers
1	2

Baby Boyd

Jaxon Boyd got so annoyed
When his parents wouldn't agree with him
About the choice of the baby's name.
(They named him *James*
And they'll call him *Jim*.)
Jax had made it very plain
That his brother's name should be
Bruce Wayne ...
(or *Clark Kent* or *Peter Parker*).

Coach Brewster

Grandy came to meet my coach.
When I introduced her,
He said, "How're ya doin', *kid*?"
She said, "How do you do, *sir*."

Mr. Cool

When I decorate my Grandad
With jewelry and bling,
He keeps looking at the football game
And doesn't say a thing.

Rained In

The attic calls on rainy days
And, under the gable roof,
We hear the raindrops pelting down
But we are waterproof.

Nicknames

Nick's great-grandmother is neat.
She always has great food to eat.
She keeps a lot on her pantry shelf
And Nick knows he can help himself.
She calls him her *Super Snacker*.
He calls her his *Great-Gram Cracker*.

Out of Touch

While Grandy visits Mrs. King,
I wait out in the grass
So then I can't break anything.
Her house is very *glass*.

Competition

When Dakotah Brown
Moved into town
With her hair in a long, black braid
And she rode her Indian pony
In the Jubilee Parade
And all the boys in town lined up
To ride in her canoe,
Susan Blair, right then and there,
Changed her name to *Sioux* ...
Or it might have had a catchy flair
To call herself *Apache* Blair.

Brad's Room

Brad wants to paint his bedroom
But he can't convince his Dad
That he and his friends can do it.
They want to paint it plaid.
His father says the plaid idea
Is a really, really bad idea.

Down Under

In Australia
Words and meanings are in sync.
A dog is called a "woofer"
And a child's a "kiddiewink."
You love to hear their accents
And the way they talk to you.
They say, "G'day" and "Cheerio"
And "Ta" and "Toodle-oo."
(That means thank you and goodbye.)

Grandad says:
"Well, I'll be gobsmacked!"
(Amazed and surprised)

Sara Ann

Sara Ann Samantha Hill
Has a voice so shrieking shrill
It puts your teeth on red alert
And makes your ears and eyeballs hurt.
John likes Mary Margalo
Who says soft things like, "Marshmallow."

Big Wheels

When Daisy Clark moved to Center Park,
Mike was the first to meet her.
He rode his tricycle next door
And rushed right up to greet her.
Daisy smiled and acted sweet
But then the ten-speed bikes
Came driving up the driveway
And parked right next to Mike's.
Mike got on his tricycle
And went home to his toys.
He said, "She really liked me
'til she met the other boys."

Suite Dreams

Kim and Tim are identical twins
But they don't agree when it comes to inns.
Tim would like it best if the family went
On a vacation in a tent.
Kimmie thought it would be neat
To reserve a gorgeous penthouse suite
In a lavish, posh hotel
But Mother chose a good motel
And Dad said, "Yes, that would be cool
IF it had a swimming pool
And a free breakfast."

Deep Six

When Ben was only five years old,
Life seemed so simple then
But now he thinks and thinks and thinks
And then he thinks again.
He is not sure of anything.
His head keeps playing tricks.
He wonders about everything.
It's harder to be six.

Finding Missing Linc
(In Pennsylvania)

Martha Washington is our cat.
She is fat and pretty.
Her husband is George Washington
And Lincoln is their kitty.
Lincoln's always getting lost
But gets back home, I guess,
Because, printed on his collar,
Is our Gettysburg address.

Droopy Drew

Drew couldn't help with the camping gear.
He sat in the shade instead
And watched us work and sipped root beer.
He had *arm bone droop*, he said.

Mirror Image

If I had a mirror
I would happily
Hold it right up to your face
So that you could see
How bad you look
When you are cross
And hollering at me.

The Fishing Lesson

I was out in a boat with Grandad Blake
Late last Sunday at the lake.
He took me out to grant my wish
And show me how to catch a fish.
It was a chance to ask about
Bass and perch and speckled trout
And if we caught one, could we cook it
If we were smart enough to hook it?
And I used all kinds of fishing terms
Like *rods* and *reels* and *lures* and *worms*.
He said if I wanted to get my wish,
That I should just shut up and fish.
He was grinning when he said it
But it didn't take me long to get it.

Beth

Beth built a snowman
And then, she admits,
She warmed cold hands
In her Dad's armpits.

Alexis

I'm thinking of making some noise today,
Blow horns or ring a bell.
Maybe I'll play with the boys today
And run around and yell.
Maybe I'll sing in a louder voice
To be heard in my little world.
Maybe I'll try it...
But I'm really a quiet
Little girl.

Valentine

My sister made a big red heart
But it wasn't filled with candy.
It had a message for the special one
That the rest of us call "Grandy".

Flip Flop

Jill had a gymnast for a sitter
Who could do amazing tricks.
She had baby sat for Jillian
Since Jillian was six
But once an older sitter came
When Mom went on a trip
And Jill was disappointed
That she couldn't do a flip.

She couldn't even do a back flip, Mom!
Don't call HER again!

Paul

With his head poked in the bushes
And on his hands and knees,
My brother, Paul, ignores us all
And talks to bumblebees.

Don't try this at home!

Archie

Archie Ryan has red hair
And everyone called him "Red"
Until he moved to Australia
Where they call him "Blue" instead.
I can't imagine why they do
But they nickname every redhead "Blue".
Doesn' t that seem strange to you?

G'Day, Blue !

Hush Money

We were having a yelling contest
To see whose voice was strongest
Until Grandy offered a dollar to
The one who kept quiet longest.

Shhhhhhhh!

Swing Dancing

Jan stepped out of the sandbox
And began to dance and glide.
She did dips and kicks and pirouettes
Around the swing and slide.
Two kids on the seesaw watched
And one on monkey bars
Said, "I guess she must be practicing
For *Dancing with the Stars*."

Grandy Says (to Rover):

Don't stick out your tongue at me.
I don't want to view it.
You should only stick your tongue out
When the vet tells you to do it.

Favorites

In Shay's side of the crayon box,
She keeps *Electric Lime*
And *Crimson* and *Magenta*
To use them all the time
But *Bubble Gum* and *Amethyst*
Are her favorites, too,
And *Chartreuse* and *Lavender*
And any shade of blue.
Matt just colors battleships
And soldiers every day
So ...
He keeps the *Camouflage* and *Khaki*
And the *Olive Drab* and *Gray*.

Holy Kangaroo!

A *chalkie* is a teacher
And a *clacker* is a tooth.
A *flutterby's* a butterfly,
A bathroom is a *toot*.
A *bubbler* is a fountain
And a *bugle* is a nose.
It would seem *bloody* funny
To say any one of those...

Unless you were in Australia.

Mitchell

When he's *ON*, he's tons of fun
But he doesn't know when to stop.
We'd never tell his Dad or Mom
Or a teacher or a cop.
We don 't want to quit on him
Or run away or sit on him
Because he's such a clown.
Grandy says that our friend, Mitch,
Really needs a dimmer switch
And *that* might calm him down.

Never-Full Nelson

Nelson Adams liked to eat
And could think of little else.
He especially liked to eat anything sweet
And one day little Nels
Went to visit Santa Claus
Who asked with twinkling eye,
"What do you want for Christmas?"
And Nels said, "Apple pie."

Old Faithful

We've had the car since I was born,
The only ride I've had.
Now they've decided to trade it in
On a new car for my Dad.
Everyone was happy
So I didn't want to cry
But I went out in the driveway
And patted it goodbye.

Concession Confession

I really like the movies
But sometimes when I go,
I really like the popcorn
Even better than the show.

Cold Duck

Pat has a cozy feather quilt
And she thinks it's ducky
But there is a chilly duck somewhere
Who isn't quite as lucky.

The Bouncer

We had a life-size punch balloon
That stood on cardboard feet.
When we punched it
Around our living room,
Mom punched it down the street.

Boing, boing, boing!

St. Patrick's Day

It's March seventeen.
Time to wear a green hat,
Green socks and shamrocks
To honor St. Pat.
Eat a green cupcake.
Chew some green gum.
Drink a green milkshake.
Beat a green drum.
But ...
You'd better be careful
On March seventeen.
If you eat too much green stuff,
You might turn green!

color him green

The Phone Call

Candy Carter called me up
And I didn't know what to do.
I passed the phone to my brother
And said, "Johnny, it's for you."

(Not so) Smart Alec

When Alec visited Aunt Ruth,
He broke a vase and hid it.
Although he should have told the truth,
He said:

the butler did it!

Aunt Ruth doesn't even have a butler.

Fiascos

Today I made cookies to send you from me.
I followed the recipe right to the "T",
Preheated the oven, watched all the clocks,
Baked for twelve minutes,
Made chocolate rocks.

Sign Language

Mom said to Dad,
"Where are we, dear?
I don't recognize this town."
(We were out on Sunday
Just driving all around).
Noah said, "It's *Trash Can*,"
And it made my mother smile.
"No kidding Mom, I saw the sign ..."

TRASH CAN

1/2 MILE

Couch Potato Chip

Chip O'Dell wasn't feeling well
But he didn't stay in bed.
He went downstairs to the TV room
To the pull-out couch instead.
All day long he blew his nose
And Chip and his Irish setter
Cuddled up and watched the shows
Until Chip was feeling better. *

*more chipper

The Wish List

A tiara, a tutu and a magic wand
Could produce such a special effect
Chris put them all on her Christmas list.
Was that too much to expect?
She mentioned all three to Santa Claus
When she climbed up on his knee
And he seemed to think that they *might* be pink
And they *might* be under her tree.

He didn't seem so sure about the Chihuahua.

Don Q. and the Cookies la Muncha

High up on the pantry shelf
Is where the cookies are.
Donnie climbed up by himself
And reached
The unreachable jar.

Rome Aroma

I *love* Italian restaurants
And would *love* to go to Rome
But I realize that Italy
Is pretty far from home.
I guess it's not a good idea.
I'll be too far away there
And, if they eat pizza every day,
I'll probably just stay there.

The Taylor Twins

They look the same.
They walk the same.
They talk the very same way
And
Their very same front tooth fell out
On the very same day.

Short Sighted

When I grow up, Diana smiled,
I have always hoped that I'll
Be tall.
I'm sick of seeing stumps of trees
And window sills and peoples' knees
And never seeing tops of things
At all.

Gravy Strain

When Mom thickens the gravy
And the flour gets into clumps,
I ask her not to strain it
Because I *like* the lumps
But she can 't please everybody
And she gets a little grumpy
When Dad says, "Well, it tastes OK
But it' s a little lumpy."

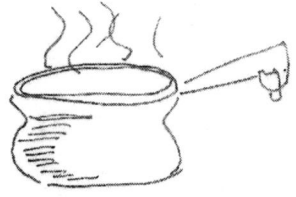

Comic Belief

Veronica told Marty Cook
She was going to give me a comic book.
Marty told me right away
What her gift would be on my party day.
Veronica, smiling very sweetly,
Fooled the two of us completely.

Veronica
Gave me a harmonica

Jolly Roger (On Halloween)

He wore high black boots and a pirate hat
And a cardboard dirk (that's a dagger),
Had a parrot, a plume and a black eye patch,
A "HO, HO, HO" and a swagger,
Mumbled and grumbled, "Avast ye swabs!"
As he collected swag
And gold doubloons and candy bars
In his trick-or-treating bag.
"This is so much fun," he said to Frank,
"Unless they make me walk a plank."

Hurt But Hungry Jack

Jack fell off the Johnson's wall
And landed on a boulder.
He landed with sufficient force
To dislocate his shoulder.
In pain and in the ambulance,
He asked the EMTs,
"On the way to the hospital,
Can I get a burger, please?"

The Time Capsule

We buried it beside the brook
With pictures that we drew
And a note that said we put it there
In 1492.
One picture was three sailing ships
Upon the bounding main
And another was a picture
Of the king and queen of Spain.
Note said: "I finally got here
And I thank you, Isabella.
Because of you and Ferdinand,
I am a happy fella.
But ...
You really gave me dinky ships
And not a Spanish galleon
So I claimed the land for Italy
Because I am Italian."

With the chance of changing history,
Timothy signed it *Christopher C.*

High School Flashback

The limo came and picked him up
And we watched Dad and Mom
Stand a long time in the doorway
When Zack went to the Prom.
"They can close the door," I said to Gertie.
"Zack won't be back 'til eleven-thirty."

The Nap Trap

Sometimes in the afternoon
In Grandy's leather chair
We sit and read together
And I really like it there.
Sometimes in the afternoon
Instead of counting sheep
I read to her and she reads to me
Until we fall asleep.

Baby Sister Janet

She can't talk yet but she sings a lot
In a language no one's heard.
It' s a funny sound like a wind-up toy
Or a squeaky little bird.
We can't understand a word she sings
Or the tune that she likes to hum.
My friend, Dee, keeps asking me,
"What planet is Janet from?"

Our Prize

We always called her "Granny"
But lately Granny Ford
Wants to be called "Grammy"
So she'll feel like an award.

Grandy Says:

Let's keep saying, "Hello"
And, "Good Morning"
And, "How Are You?"
And, "Happy Birthday."
Let's not say, "Goodbye"
Or, "So Long"
Or anything like that.
Let's keep saying,

Hello!

CPSIA information can be obtained at www.ICGtesting.com
Printed in the USA
LVOW08s0004020215

425281LV00001B/18/P